ATTACK OF THE 50-FOOT FLY GUY

Tedd Arnold

Cartwheel Books

An Imprint of Scholastic Inc.

This, my 100th book, I dedicate to my loving wife, Carol, who inspired this career of mine in the first place.

Library of Congress Cataloging-in-Publication Data available

ISBN 978-1-338-56626-0

10 9 8 7 6 5 4 3 2 1   19 20 21 22 23

Printed in Malaysia 108

First edition, September 2019

Book design by Kirk Benshoff

A boy had a pet fly.
He named him Fly Guy.
Fly Guy could say
the boy's name —

Chapter 1

Once, when Fly Guy woke up,
Buzz was already at school.
Mom and Dad were at work.
So, Fly Guy went out for
breakfast.

He nibbled.

He snacked.

He gobbled.

Fly Guy was still hungry.
He smelled something
interesting. He followed his
nose.

Fly Guy found a strange can of garbage. It tasted weird.

Fly Guy felt sick.
He flew back home and fell
asleep on Buzz's bed.

Chapter 2

Later, Buzz came home from school. His bed was between two trees!

"Where's my house?" asked Buzz.

Buzz looked up. Fly Guy
looked down.

"Fly Guy!" cried Buzz.

"My house is on your head!"

"I have the best idea," said Buzz.
"Put my house down and give
me a ride!"

EATZZ!

"If you're hungry," said Buzz, "we can go back to the house and eat."

Chapter 3

"This is not good, Fly Guy," said Buzz. "Let's figure it out. What did you do today that made you so big?"

"So, you went out to eat?" asked Buzz.

Buzz looked down below.
The garbage truck and a
police car were following them.

"Maybe it was something you ate," said Buzz. "Take me where you went to eat."

Fly Guy took Buzz to where he nibbled.

And where he snacked.

And where he gobbled.

The garbage truck and more
police cars were coming. "Any
other place?" asked Buzz.

Fly Guy flew to the strange garbage can. Just then, a scientist was taking out some garbage.

"Oh my!" said the scientist.
Buzz yelled, "Can you fix
Fly Guy?"

"No problem," said the scientist. "Come down here and stick out your tongue. This might taste a little weird."

Suddenly, the garbage truck and police cars came around the corner, followed by a helicopter, army tanks, and jets.

The army general shouted,
"Where's the 50-foot monster?"

"No monsters here," said Buzz.
"Just my little pet fly."

The army general said,
"Well, we wouldn't hurt a fly!"

Then everyone went home.

"That was fun, Fly Guy!" said Buzz.
"What do you want to do now?"